Fascinating Short Stories Of Kids Who Dare To Be Different

* * *

Dally Perry

Cover Design by
Victichy

SMARTARROW PUBLISHER

ISBN 978-1-959581-20-8

Printed in the United States of America

Contents

For Valen, Vishal, and Videl.

This Fascinating Short Stories

For Kids Belongs to

* * *

1

Introduction

Stories have been known to help raise kids to be more positive minded and groomed to grow up to become better people. The spread of negative messages on various channels grows by the day and kids get to see and hear these messages. It would only be a wise move to have inspiring and positive stories to guide children in the right path and help them see a different aspect of life that exist that isn't often projected for the world to see.

Inspiring and positive stories helps kids to believe more in themselves, thus the reason for the collection of this inspiring short stories of individuals who were brave enough to be distinct. This was shown in their achievements in spite their poverty-stricken background, physical and mental challenges and a whole of limitations.

Every one of these people overcame adversities and changed their world, and today they have built ways for others to live better lives. Each and every one of them worked very hard and sustained self-confidence, even when they were doubted by others or told that their dreams would not be achieved.

This book is good for children who are looking for inspirational and fun stories who have resolved to stand out positively. Here they can find stories of strong role models who impacted their world. These stories help children know that it is never too late to begin to make a difference in their various sectors, their aspirations, in their goal and their dreams. Children are the masters of their own destinies.

These stories reveals that you can overcome whatever obstacles may lie ahead, you should never give up on your dreams. In simple terms, this inspiring book is about the potential inside of everyone one of us to enable us chase our dreams and shape our own paths. It is this treasure we get to cherish for eternity with our loved ones.

Whether you are a boy or a girl, it's our hope that these stories inspire you greatly to know and internalize that you can make a difference as well.

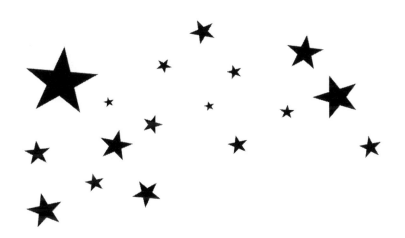

*
 *
*   *

2

LOVE

The Master And His Inquisitive Disciples

Detachment brings peace of mind

There was once a good Master who had obedient disciples. These disciples were fond of asking their Master so many questions about what is right and what is wrong. Often times these disciples will end up getting obvious responses, but this didn't stop them from asking their dear Master more and more inquiries. At times, the disciples will arrive at very vague answers. The Master made it a point of duty not to take part in his disciple's discussions, especially whenever he is around.

One funny day, one of his disciples asked him if it was in order to kill someone who seeks to kill him first or if it was wrong at the same time.

The Master responded, "How should I possibly know the answer to that?" The stunned disciple responded, "How then can we know our right from our wrong?" The Master then gave a response that cleared the air to his disciples. He told them saying, "While you are alive, be totally dead to yourself. Then act as you deem fit and then your actions will always be right."

This story teaches us that, 'While you are still alive, being dead to oneself' talks about detachment. Ironically, when there isn't an attachment to something, it has a way of not allowing you to think about manipulating/scheming, or the thoughts to commit any mistake will be unlikely. Detachment brings about a strange but fulfilling state of peace in the mind. When a person's mind is calm and serene, he isn't prone to committing any sin.

The Optician Who Made A Difference

Love everybody and offer unbiased support to them

Once upon a time, there lived a great optician, he was a cheerful fellow, a philanthropist who does well and was loved by so many people. He was greatly esteemed because he was able to carry out his profession in the most admirable manner. The optician fell in love with a little blind boy who assisted his poor father to sell newspapers just around the corner of the street where he lives. The little blind boy's name was Marvin; he was a bright boy with a positive spirit. One would hardly know he was blind until you look very close. One faithful day, the optician asked Marvin, "Would you like me to cure your eyes so that you can see and play around like other kids?"

Marvin was sad and responded saying that he doesn't have what it will take to pay the revered optician, and besides his father was very poor and won't be able to pay for the operation. The doctor told little Marvin that he will do it out of love and not for the money.

Marvin then replied to the doctor saying, "Oh my, Doctor, that would make me so happy." The doctor got Marvin ready for the eye surgery, in the operating room before Marvin was injected with anesthesia, he asked for an opportunity to pray and was granted. Marvin prayed that God grants the doctor long life so that he will be able to save other people who are less privileged like himself. The prayer got the doctor emotional and he told Marvin, "Marvin, in my twenty-five years as an optician, I have operated on many people of very high status and I have been paid very handsomely for my services. But I haven't gotten so much satisfaction for doing what I love to do best, unlike haven decided to operate on your eyes, you give me so much fulfillment!"

The doctor's act of love was a rarity because that was an expensive surgery, but he still chose to be different in a world where nothing is free and gave a poor little boy an opportunity to live the life he had always dreamt of. In truth, a modest act of love and service without hoping for any reward in return is greater than any amount of money.

Face Your Worst Fears

Love doesn't victimize

A while back, there was a period when racial discrimination thrived to a large extent against black people all over the world and these special races of people were looked down on as seen as lesser humans. There were constant and severe death threats to black people who lived in perpetual fear for a long time, for their dear lives and for that of their loved ones just, because of the color of their skin.

During these trying times, there was a church that had a black priest presiding over the church. Daily, he will hold masses for every single person, this made him loved and highly esteemed by a lot of people. One time, the church was attacked by some troublemakers who intended to set the church ablaze just because it was run by a black priest. The miscreants went for the priest with the intent of hurting him, he stepped back and told them...

"If you don't like me because I am ignorant, you can send me to a school so I can get an education. If you don't like me because I am untidy, you can teach me how to wash myself clean. If you don't like me because of my unsocial habits, you can teach me how to live more sociable in society. But if you don't like me because of my skin color, then I will have to refer you to God who made me this way."

The priest was bold enough to face his worst fears. He said the obvious truth in the face of imminent hurt or worse still – death! The color of our skin is a thing we all are born with as humans and nothing can help change that. There isn't any reason acceptable enough for discrimination of any kind, talk more of it being racial... it's an inexcusable injustice meted out on an individual's humanity.

Leo The Miser

Greed slows you down, be generous, it's a show of affection

Once upon a time, there lived a very stingy man named Leo in Austria, Vienna who chose not to get married so he doesn't have to share his hard-earned money with his kids, his wife, or his family as a whole.

Leo had an underground cellar in his home where he keeps all his treasures. Leo goes up there frequently and every night to admire his treasures before going to bed. He saves daily just to increase his treasures.

One time, Leo wasn't seen for many days and then days turned into months and the local police spread the word all over the town of the strange disappearance of Leo.

As there wasn't anyone to come forward to claim his property and house, it was converted to that of the Government and was later sold off to a wealthy man in the area for a very handsome price. After some time, one day when the new owner of Leo's home was renovating the home to suit his taste, he discovered an underground vault and the sight shook him to his bones. He found Leo the miser decomposing away among his glittering gold and jewels. In Leo's mouth, there was a candle piece he was eating just to compress his hunger. Leo had so much wealth but he lived on candles just to keep growing his treasures. That was a very stupid move that cost him his life.

True wealth lies in how many people's life you touched positively and not in what you own or the amount of wealth you have piled up in one storehouse. Greed limits one, don't let greed hold you back from achieving all the great things you have lined up for yourself. You can do great things.

Affectionate Correction

Be the example you preach

The Browns' were a popular family in their small villa due to the enormous farmlands they used for cultivating several crops for sale and for their home use. They had a grown-up son named David who was 20 years old. The Browns lived a bit far from the city and they owned a large part of the land.

One good day, David and his dad took a drive to the city to attend some business meetings and to get some groceries. David's dad allowed him to drive and he was so excited that his father trusts him to drive them safely to the city which was some miles away.

On their way to the city, David's dad discovered that the car will need some repairs, so he told David to drop him at his meeting spot and head on to the mechanic garage to get the car scanned and fixed. So, David dropped his dad off for his meeting and went straight to the mechanic's place, with the instruction to have the car picked up at 3.00 pm so he can get his father at 3.30 pm, and then they both can return home together. David dropped the car at the mechanic's garage, he finished shopping for all the groceries as quickly as possible and then head directly to the movies to watch his favorite series at the cinemas. David was carried away with the series he went to watch that he lost track of the time and it was past 4 pm already.

David dashed off to the mechanic and picked up the car and headed off quickly to get his father who was already anxious as to where his son had been for over an hour ago while he waited. David wasn't aware that his dad had already called the mechanic over the phone at 3.00 pm who told him that his son hadn't come to pick up the car yet and that the car repair was done since 2.30 pm. David's father asked him why he was late and David lied to his father that the mechanic has kept him waiting as he wasn't done with the car till this late, instead of telling his father the truth he went to the movies'.

David's dad was upset that his son didn't trust him enough to tell him the truth about where he had been and chose to tell him a lie instead. So, he decided to punish David for telling a lie, but with love. The dad told David that he made a mistake in the way he raised him up, so to correct the lapses in the failure in his upbringing he will teach him a lesson by him walking back home from the city to their home in the villa.

It was night and there was no street light on the road. David's father stumbled a lot of times on the road and David felt ashamed of himself. Walking from the city, a lot of people kept looking at David in the car while his father walked on food and he felt more ashamed of himself as he drove slowly behind his father. They got home five hours later. Instead of punishing his son David, he chose to punish himself which was a rare act that touched David's heart to repentance from future lies. This was a fundamental way of teaching a lesson that can be adopted by fellow parents.

The Cold Hands Of Karma

Choose your own path in life

Once upon a time, there lived a little boy and girl born into the loving arms of their parents – Brighton's. These kids were named Hansel and Gretel as they were twins. As they grew up, they had two more siblings and their parents loved them very much. This family was an envy of many in the community, they served as models to families going through marital challenges. In fact, one time, a couple was brave enough to walk into their home to tell them how watching their marriage helped them to work out their own marital issues and they have Hansel and Gretel's parents to thank for that divine intervention; now they are happier and can't imagine life with any other person.

As the years passed, the Brighton's lost touch with their early love, and they quarreled almost every day till they decided to part ways. This incident broke the hearts of many people in their neighborhood and they did their very best to reconcile Mr. and Mrs. Brighton, but nothing seemed to work.

One day, Hansel and Gretel asked their mom what happened to their parent's love and how come it died. Their mom told them saying, "Kids, I have been covering your day for so long. He has been hitting me but I keep wearing makeup early in the mornings so you all don't get to see the black eyes. I have been enduring many things from your dad just to be able to stay here and take good care of you all and to maintain that perfect family stereotype to people in our community who look up to us so much, but we can't lie to ourselves again, we feel out of love some years ago after birthing the both of you, then the beating began, but now I can't take anymore beating."

The twins were very sad on hearing from their mom, they began to recall that they often have some brown substance on their school uniforms, but they asked their mom because she always works very hard to get them ready for school. So that goes to explain what that brown stain was, but they never thought their mom was ever wearing makeup because it would be very tiring to consistently keep up such an act, but their mom did!

A few weeks after their divorce, Mr. Brighton got married to his fling causing his former marriage to fail. This singular act hurt Hansel and Gretel a great deal, they swore to protect their mom come what may and vowed to never get married in life, they told their mum that true love does not exist except in fairy tales.

This decision weighed their mom down and she kept talking them not to choose such a path and told them they can still fall in love and find a great partner. But the twins were still blinded by how their father treated their mom poorly, ran off to marry another, and forgot totally about them. The twins grew up to be very wealthy and gave their mom the best of life, unfortunately, their mom developed a brain tumor that had already gotten cancerous to a large extent and was on her death bed. She made the twins promise her that they will open their minds to the world of love and live a life different from that of their fathers'.

Before their mom finally gave up the ghost, they both found beautiful partners, and their father returned apologizing that he didn't know what came over him and he recounted how his second wife took all his wealth and fled to marry her high school sweetheart. This was a case of karma serving someone a cold dish of pain. I would say Mr. Brighton deserves what he got, but what I can say is that we all have the pen to write the events that happen in our lives to a large extent. We shouldn't choose a path because of an extended hurt, do things differently, life isn't only filled with bad people, there are still lovely people and you and I are one of them; so let's spread that positive vibe around.

COURAGE

The Telephone Operator Who Saved The Day

True courage stands the test of time

Many years ago, Mrs. J Brookes, a telephone operator of Folsom, New Mexico informed residents of the hills to run for their dear lives due to the imminent flood that was racing at great speed to engulf the valley. Close to fifty families had their lives saved due to the rare act of bravery displayed by a fragile elderly woman.

Her magnificent show of courage is worthy of emulation. Mrs. Brookes used her only opportunity to save herself and instead used it to warn others of the coming danger via calls to subscribers knowing fully well that she was going to die if she stayed back to warn the community.

True courage is tested in trying times when you totally choose others over yourself even when it is very uncomfortable for you – that's courage in its undiluted form.

Dereck The Immature Grown-Up

True courage lays in the truth

Dereck was 14 years old now and was in college. He saw himself as an adult and began to do very naughty things that were way above his age grade. He started drinking, smoking, and flirting around with underage girls.

Dereck assumed that these were his highest adulthood conquests. Each night, Dereck comes back home very late, and then he will tell a lie to his parents as to why he returned late.

One night, when Dereck came back home again, his dad welcomed him home with an embrace, putting his arms around Dereck's shoulders, and inquired of him, "Dereck, when do you think one becomes a grown-up?" Dereck was silent and could not respond to his dad that drinking, smoking, and flirting with girls are the factors that make an individual a grown-up. His dad noticed how taciturn Dereck became immediately he asked that question and then told him; "An individual could be said to be a grown-up the moment he becomes conscious of how pointlessness it is to tell lies to anyone about whatsoever."

Only an immature mind tells lies, and it is also cowardice to not be able, to tell the truth about a situation. The truth requires a high level of courage, and courage entails being an adult.

Two Wishes Before I Die

Growth is a journey

Once upon a time, a Buddha passed by a jungle that was said to be controlled by an evil bandit called Bangumin. Unfortunately, the Buddha was captured before he could make it by the jungle and was threatened with death by the evil bandits.

The Buddha appealed to the bandits to grant him two wishes so he said to them; "Please be good enough to grant me two wishes before killing me. First, cut down the branch of that tree," the Buddha said as he pointed to the tree nearby. The bandits swung their swords just once and the tree's branch was off on the ground. The bandits asked the Buddhist, "Any other request?" The Buddhist said again, "Put the branch back together with the tree again." The bandits mocked the Buddhist saying, "You must be crazy to think that anyone could a thing like that."

The Buddha answered and said, "On the contrary, you are insane if you ever think you are superior because you can inflict injury and destroy lives. This wise response of the Buddhists disarmed the bandits and they went their way without hurting the Buddhists.

Advancement and progress happen in silence. Destruction is often followed by a loud noise. The construction of an edifice is a process of silence. The demolition of a building is followed by a roaring sound. Growth takes some time to gain, like the advancement of a tree. Damage happens in no time like that hacking down a tree.

The Great Emperor And His Steadfast Senate

Courage warms the heart

A long time ago, far away in Russia, the Emperor named Peter the Great was childless for many years without a child and he kept praying and praying to have at least one child to call his own as he wasn't getting any younger. After many years of waiting, the Emperor was blessed with a healthy son and the whole kingdom was joyful for this rare gift. But their joy was short-lived as the child few days after he was born. Everyone was sad,, the boy's mother was broken into several pieces and it was hard to console her at this point. The Emperor wore sack clothes and wept for days too. He locked himself up for many days so that he could starve to death.

Peter The Great gave a scary decree that if anyone bothers his retirement that person would be put to death immediately, be it, anyone. The senate gathered to talk about the way forward to rescue their Emperor from not killing himself. One of the Emperor's ministers named Dologorouki volunteered to rescue their leader from certain death. Dologorouki bravely went to the Emperor's room and knocked for him to open up, but the Emperor caused with a terrible tone and said; "Whoever you are, disappears from here or I will open the door and knock out your brains!"

The senate, Dologorouki responded in a resolute manner and said, "Open I say, it is my duty as the senate to find out who the Emperor wishes to name as the Emperor in your

Excellency's absence as you have now retired permanently."

The Emperor unlocked the door, came out of his morning clothes, and hugged the senate. The Czar listened to his dedicated courtier's counsel and so he went back to rule over his people.

Dologorouki showed bravery that won the heart of the Emperor. A quote by Dr. Alexis Carrel says: "Nature does not pity those who are lazy or feeble-minded. She favors those who are sober, alert, intelligent, and enthusiastic; most of all, those who dare to take risks and who possess the will to succeed. She smiles at those who are ready to live hard and dangerously. Whoever refuses to take risks pays the penalty of loss of life in one form or another."

Dare To Change Your World

WHAT ARE THE THINGS YOU DESIRE IN LIFE?

Virtue is incomparable

Phillip had three grown-up kids. One faithful day, Phillip spoke to all of his kids and chose to test them so that he can get to know them. He told them to pick anything they wanted the most in life.

The first child who is a son said he wanted money. The second child is a daughter and she said wanted beauty. The third child who is a son said he wanted wisdom.

The kids' father responded to them all three that all they have asked for and desired all have no weight and no value.

Their father told them that there is only one thing in life with the highest value and it is a virtue. Virtue cannot be compared to anything else in life, and five great factors that make up virtue which is; kindness, sincerity, courtesy, earnestness, and magnanimity.

Kindness and earnestness can help you succeed, sincerity helps men trust you more, courtesy helps you stay away from insults, and with magnanimity, you get to win everything.

Do Good And Be Good

Goodness comes from healthy thoughts and intentions

A renowned school in Nashville had a Moral Science teacher who was great in her craft. One day this teacher told her students in the last period of class to file out of the class carefully and go and be good as they retired home. The kids were happy to carry out the exercise and returned one by one with their different experiences of good being expressed to their fellow humans.

One student who went out after school had closed distributed gifts to the poor people living on his street and assisted many others who were in need of one help or the other. The following day, he told his teacher of his good deed, but his teacher was far from being impressed after all the things he told her he did.

The student was confused at this point and wondered if he didn't get the correct memo of what the teacher told them to do. The teacher saw her student's facial expression and then told him "I asked you to be good and not to do good! They are two different things."

The teacher explained to her student that people do good things but that doesn't make them good individuals. She said people give gifts and beautiful things to help the poor and less privileged just for the show of it without genuinely intending to assist the needy.

Tony The Shrewd Businessman

Be dedicated to the end

Tony was a very successful but shrewd businessman. Unfortunately, he was on his deathbed and was close to his end. On his deathbed, his family had gathered around him very sad. Tony asked if his eldest son was present in his sick bed and they acknowledged that he was. Tony then asked about his second son and they affirmed that he was there. Tony wanted to know if his other students were present too and he got a positive reply.

Suddenly Tony got upset when he discovered that he was surrounded by his entire family and they wondered what wrong they had done. Tony could hold it in, gathered some energy, and shouted at everyone saying, "If everyone is here by me, who then is taking care of my estates?"

This was a very weird question but that goes to show that Tony the shrewd businessman was disciplined till his death. Tony's dedication to his business earned him so much wealth that even while he was dying, he still gave credence to the factor that helped him become a household name.

The Lawyer With A Large Heart

Have a big heart

One time, a cornfield farmer named Evan had issues with his neighbor because of the line demarcating their farms. It began as a little issue and then gravitated into a big issue. Evan escalated the matter to the lawyer Milton in other to file a case against his neighbor.

To his amazement, Evans' neighbor also came with the same intent of filing a petition against Evans to Milton. Milton then told them both saying, "If the both of you go on fighting like this, it will lead to the hatred that will outlast many generations which is a very bad thing.

Milton told Evan and his neighbor that the both of them should settle out of court and settle at a compromise but both farmers were too stubborn and hated the idea Milton proposed for their settlement. After much back and forth, both farmers saw reasons with Milton to compromise and settle the challenge out of court.

Milton got them to cooperate by telling the two farmers to sit in his office so that he can attend to a stranger outside and still advised them to settle their differences harmoniously. So Milton locked the door to his office so he doesn't interrupt them with his own discussion outside, thereby leaving both farmers to themselves. Milton returned later in the afternoon to meet the two men conversing with each other. They had spent too much time alone to not speak with each other, and during their discussion they resolved to settle out of court as their best option. So, before Lincoln came, both farmers had gotten the matter sorted.

Milton had a large heart, he wasn't all about the money which he would be paid for petitioning those farmers, and instead, he went all out to help them.

Tetsugen The Angel Without Wings

Elevate others

A long time ago, there lived a student of Zen in Japan named Tetsugen, who spearheaded the almighty undertaking of the production of the first complete woodcut edition of about 60,000 pieces of the Chinese Buddhist sutras in Japan. Before this time, the sutras were only available in the Chinese language.

Tetsugen journeyed far and wide in Japan to get resources for this venture. Some rich people gave him a hundred pieces of gold, and some others offered him a little amount of money, but Tetsugen in his usual fashion expressed the same level of gratitude to each benefactor irrespective of the amount donated. Later after over ten long years of journey, he decided to take the funds needed for the job. At that juncture, the river Uji spilled over and thousands of people had to starve as they didn't have any more food and shelter. Tetsugen had to make a hard decision that was detrimental to his ongoing project, he had to spend all his project money to help the less privileged people. Tetsugen started working on raising a new set of funds again. It took several years before he got the funds needed to execute his project.

Yet again, it took many years for Tetsugen to get the money he needed, then another challenge crept in. It was a wicked epidemic that spread very quickly all over the country and began to claim lives without any permission. Tetsugen had no other option than to give the funds he had gathered for many years for the execution of his project to render help to the dying people.

Later Tetsugen set out again on his journey in search of funds for his project, it was until twenty years later that Tetsugen's dream saw the light of day. What Tetsugen did went down in history, today the printing house that published his first edition of the sutras is displayed at the Obaku Monastery in Kyoto. History has it that Tetsugen rolled out three editions of the sutras in totality. The first two editions of the sutras are the financial assistance he presented to people affected and distraught by the flood and the epidemic. This rare act of kindness is taken as invisible editions of the book, which are far more superior to the third one which we all can see and hold.

Tetsugen did a unique thing that is a difficult task to carry out, he served individuals going through challenges that had nowhere else to go, and this was far more than publishing any kind of book.

Destiny The Woodcutter And The Wise Monk

Be Content

There was once a woodcutter who lived in a faraway village called Destiny. He was very poor and couldn't make ends meet, so he began cutting down trees in forests and selling the wood in the town for money. On one faithful day, Destiny saw a monk meditating somewhere in the forest where he usually cut down his trees for sale.

Destiny chose to speak to the monk to get his advice on how to earn more money so his life can change for the better. The Monk was still meditating when Destiny approached him, when the monk opened his eyes, Destiny asked him the ways he can earn more.

The monk encouraged Destiny to go deeper into the forest so he can make a month's worth of food in just a day's work. Destiny took the monk's advice and moved deeper into the forest and discovered sandalwood trees. Destiny cut them and sold them, he made so much more than what he had ever earned before.

Destiny met the monk to appreciate him for the valuable advice he gave him. The monk said that if he can still deeper into the forest that Destiny would be able to get much more than what he made now. Destiny decided to go much deeper into the forest and discovered a great treasure – a silver mine. Destiny then took the treasure and went to thank the monk for his words of wisdom.

Then again, the monk recommended that Destiny goes deeper still into the forest where he can see the real treasure, and then there would be no more reason to work. Destiny took the monk's advice and went deeper into the forest and this time he found a gold mine. Destiny was so happy and met the monk to express his deepest gratitude for guiding him on the right path to find such immense treasures.

Destiny asked the monk why he himself have never gone into the deepest part of the forest so that he can get the treasures as well since he knew about what the deep part of the forest held.

When Destiny asked the monk that, he said "The treasures you got will only gratify you just for a particular period of time. If you intend to be happy forever, then you have to begin an inward journey by meditating that is what I am doing."

Long-lasting joy can be gotten if you are not greedy and don't run after worldly enticements and wealth, but by constantly decreasing our wants. The monk explained that this point gives you a high form of bliss which is called the 'Samadhi' phase in Yoga.

BE THE CHANGE YOU SEEK

Use Up All Your Strength

Seeking assistance doesn't reduce you

One sunny evening, Mr. Brendan was on a stroll with his dear son. The weather was so favorable for a walk, on the way side were butterflies flying freely from one flower to the other. Nature was just beautiful to these two and they were having a great time.

On their way, they saw a big stone that blocked their way. The boy jumped to pick the stone but it was too heavy for his age. His dad then asked the son if he has used all his strength and the son said yes that he had come to the end of his strength.

The father told his son saying, "No, my son, you have not used up all your strength. You have not asked me to help you out."

Strength resides in exploring every possibility to achieve a task. This involves assisting others to assist you when the need arises. Everyone needs somebody to help them at one time or the other in life. No institution can stand without the assistance of others.

King Codrus The Selfless

Patriotism

A long time ago in the kingdom of Athens, the military had to build a sturdy defense to put away the Dorian invaders. The Dorian invaders were very sure they will defeat the Athenian warriors because they all have been instructed by their Oracle that it was either the whole of Athens perish or her king.

The Athenians were frantic about the upcoming battle and couldn't bear to think about them losing their dear king named Codrus. One night, an Athenian pauper got into the Dorian camp and intentionally picked a fight with a few of the soldiers present.

This information spread wide through the army camp, and panic erupted in the general public. By morning, the Dorians fled after remembering what the Oracle said about the battle.

The Dorians fled due to the horror they witnessed as the Athenian peasant that was killed in the camp was King Codrus disguised as a pauper – he gave his life to save the whole of his subjects.

Only a selfless king will lay down his precious life for his country. King Codrus' action is worthy of commendation, till date no one has been able to top king Codrus' act, nor has anyone been more worthy than him to wear the crown.

The Echo

The world returns whatever we give it

A little boy named Tony was playing around on a hilltop, Tony screamed asking, "Who are you?" and the echo replied to him with the same words back. Tony spoke again saying, "You are a mean boy." Again, the echo responded back to Tony with the same words he said.

Tony felt down and returned home to tell his mom his experience on the hilltop. Tony's mom told him to speak more friendly to the echo next time. She told Tony to say, "' I love you' to the echo and wait for the response he will get."

The following day, Tony went back to the top of the hill and screamed, "I love you." Then the echo responded by saying, "I love you." Tony was glad to hear the echo say that back to him.

This echo tale is the story of our life. The world we live in only reflects our reactions. If we think we are good, then we feel that the world should be good to us as well. If we are bad, we expect that the world will only dish out evil to us.

Life is like a complete circle. Everything we give to the world returns right back. So if we desire good, we have to do good and also be good.

The Animal Kingdom's Party

Self-discipline

A long time ago, all the animals in the jungle gathered for an animal party. At the party, they complained that the humans were often stealing their items. One by one all the animals were outlined how humans stole from them in their own specific ways.

The cow said that humans have taken away her milk, the hen added that her eggs were stolen away, the pigs said that their flesh was taken and the whale said that her oil was extracted, and so they went. After they all have spoken, the snail was the last one to speak, "I have something they want more than anything else in the world and would definitely take away if they could."

The snail was speaking about the time it has. Humans are in dire need of time, but it can't be taken away from the snail.

Time is very precious and one of the most valuable possessions on earth. Time cannot be borrowed from others, and it can't be borrowed from anyone.

To make total use of your life, you have to be thankful for the importance of time and self-discipline. If you are able to utilize your time effectively, you can enjoy your work and leisure. Self-discipline refers to the willpower to do carrying out the things which we are aware should be carried out, before doing the things we want to do because they are more enjoyable. Confronting tasks is better rather than procrastinating, you will mostly get enough time to do both of them. It is the time that you are spending. Gain mastery of your time first so you can gain mastery of yourself.

CREATIVITY

The Little Child From The Trenches Who Wears Potato Sacks

Don't let your past define your future

There was once a young black girl named Oprah who lived with her grandma. They both go to church together, Oprah learned to quote bible verses well till she was popularly called "Ms. Preacher." This helped her gain self-confidence and sharpened her communication skill in the media field. Oprah owes all of her achievements to her grandmother even though it was very rough for them.

To say how poor Oprah was, she had to wear potato sacks because there were no funds to get clothes.

Oprah came from the trenches, she was born by a housekeeper and got pregnant out of wedlock when she was 14 years old but the son died and then life became worse for her thereafter.

Oprah's grandma would abuse her by beating her whenever she erred. When Oprah was six years old, she went to live with her mother Vernita Lee who was always busy working and had no time to care for her.

Oprah was sexually assaulted by her uncle, cousin, and a family friend on several occasions. When she told her family, they said she lied about it. At school she was bullied and mentally abused more, she started stealing from her mum and would get away with it because she didn't watch her. Oprah found solace in the arms of abusive older men every time the quarrels began at home.

Oprah was sent to live with the man they believed was her father – Vernon Winfrey who instilled in her the value of being educated. She was enrolled in a decent school and began to evolve. She won several awards and became popular for her excellent results. She got employed temporarily at a local radio news station and then her career in media kicked start. Later she was an anchor for local TV news and their viewership improved tremendously due to her involvement in the show. This made the firm make her a co-host for a talk show and finally host her own show.

Oprah Winfrey's Show located in Chicago became the talk of the town as it featured prevalent topics in the community, news, challenges, ailments and their treatments, human right tales, and racial issues were the prevalent topics of discussion on her show. Her show further humanized actors and actresses, politicians, musicians, sports icons, and many other celebrities. Real-life situations are discussed on the show and confessions are been made based on real issues so everyone can learn one or two things from the experience of another. Today Oprah Winfrey has become a household name.

Her show was hosted for over 20 years and fetched millions of dollars for Oprah. She built her own production studio and got into other media-based achievements. It will be hard to believe that someone with her kind of past is worth about $3 billion today. Oprah is a present candidate for certifying the body's Most Influential People list, a fighter for human poverty, an activist for human rights, and an advocate for the LGBT community, children, and respect for women. Oprah has been awarded several scholarships and built schools for the less privileged in Africa.

Oprah Winfrey is a renowned talk show personality, activist for the abused, and a made entertainment tycoon. She is a prim and proper lady who is a true definition of an alpha female, intelligent, properly groomed, and graceful who focused only on the good.

Leonardo Da Vinci

Discernment

Once upon a time there lived a male scientist who also painted works of art as a measure of his impressive desire to see all that was noticeable; his name was Leonardo da Vinci.

Leonardo da Vinci was born into the rich and prominent family of his father and got a very basic education which wasn't befitting of their status. He was seen as the illegitimate son of a servant girl and a Florentine lawyer. Leonardo da Vinci didn't have a legitimate half-brother or half-sister to contest for his father's favor, and neither did he expect to be groomed as a legitimate child brought up to be a promising young man.

He learned to read and write and loved arithmetic. He didn't receive a classical education, so he didn't know any Greek or spoke any Latin. He was tall, very handsome, and looked athletic. He had a striking singing voice and was skilled at playing musical instruments. All these qualities aren't what made him a household name today, but his ability to see more than we can see. Leonardo da Vinci looked at things more intentionally and keenly.

He gained knowledge from employing his unique power of focus, and useful with the dexterity of his hand, he was able to draw. One time an art critic said many years later about Leonardo da Vinci that "He could draw, like an angel."

When Leonardo da Vinci turned fourteen, his father took him to the studio of Andrea Del Verrocchio to learn from the renowned master goldsmith, sculptor, and painter whose skill and meticulous artistry were chosen to be patronized by the Medicis, the ruling family of Florence, the capital of the early Renaissance at the time. Andrea Del Verrocchio was just the best master to mold Leonardo da Vinci to be the best artist in the world.

His education had not prepared his mind to admire the classic artworks of the Greek and Roman age when he sees one as the success of the main aesthetic, the aesthetic relived, reborn, in the Renaissance. Leonardo da Vinci would draw, paint, and sculpt life just as he saw and witnessed it with his human eye, without allowing himself to impose his observation on his art or his art the ideals of expression of the past.

In 1473 Leonardo turned twenty-one years old, and his master Verrocchio accepted a directive to do a painting of the Baptism of Christ, for the Convent of San Salvi in Florence. The drawing was done in oil, which was a rarity in Florence at the time. When the job was done, it was all shades of mastery. Its details were striking and everyone knew that Verrocchio will be very proud of his ability to reel out masterpiece upon masterpiece every time.

But this outstanding masterpiece for the Convent of San Salvi wasn't done by Verrocchio like many thought, but it was drawn by his apprentice Leonardo. This made Verrocchio come to the realization that Leonardo was more skillful and visionary than he was and that he was destined to be a more influential artist than he will ever be.

Today, we are aware that Leonardo Da Vinci successfully painted seventeen great masterpieces recognized globally, with many others yet to be completed. Some of his top works are; —The Adoration of the Magi, Saint Jerome in the Wilderness, the Louvre Virgin of the Rocks, The Last Supper, the ceiling of the Sala delle Asse, The Virgin and Child with Saint Anne, and Saint John the Baptist, The Virgin, and Child with Saint Anne and the Mona Lisa.

There was no field of inquiry Leonardo didn't chase. He became a scientist of every discipline and an artist of every standard. He was a botanist, anatomist, biologist, engineer, aerologist, astrologist, paleontologist, physicist, mechanic, sculptor, architect, mapmaker, painter, designer of pageants, and many more. Still, he wasn't satisfied. He began to read like an angry lion (voraciously).

Leonardo was also a seasoned writer and later felt that literature was a lesser art and not so sure medium of passing information. He was always ready, carrying around a pad of paper he always stuck to his belt, ever ready for a quick drawing based on observation or discovery. Scattered through his notebooks were observations of an essay on a painting that a close devotee put together after he passed away.

Thank God Leonardo's work lives after him, if not it would have been a great disaster. He didn't allow his background to dictate his outcome and soared above any educational limitation or family shame and brought honor to his craft and family at the end of the day. That's a true hero raising above the norm.

Charles Darwin The Father Of Evolution

Curiosity

Charles Darwin was known for his rare curiosity and bravery which assisted him in finding the history of nature and beginning an argument that has lasted for over 150 years now. Charles Darwin was once a playful and lazy boy. His father was Robert Darwin and he feared that his son will never become a respectable Victorian gentleman.

Charles was lazy but had a strange sense of curiosity, his father sent him off to Cambridge University as his last attempt to give him a direction in life after failing woefully in medical school.

Charles Darwin got bored of education quickly and chose to spend more of his time outdoors, walking, riding, shooting, playing with dogs, and collecting little things for his many collections. His father feared again that his son was on another irrelevant pursuit like he typically does. Charles Darwin began to collect different kinds of insects to study them, he collected various bugs for the pleasure of it.

But all of Charles wasn't a bad omen, his curiosity earned him a place as the youngest, most renowned, controversial scientist, the father of modern biology, and the man who broke down much mystery of mysteries.

Charles wasn't exactly an idle boy, unlike his father had thought of him to be, maybe just a little distracted and much of a daydreamer, but he wasn't exactly lazy. Charles was a child that never wanted to do the normal things kids would do, he only engaged in things that juggles his curiosity and intellect. Charles enjoyed only things that interested him and geometry that was taught to him by a private teacher.

Charles loved the outdoors, you need to see Charles' excitement anytime he is on summer vacation with his family in North Wales. Charles was born as the second son to Robert and Susannah Darwin on the 12th of February, 1809, in Shrewsbury, Shropshire, in the English Midlands. Charles' father was a physician and had a logical mind which influenced Charles while growing up that fed his scientific mind. Charles' paternal grandfather, Erasmus Darwin, was likewise a physician, who enjoyed a global status as a man of medicine, a poet, inventor, and a biologist.

Reverend John Stevens Henslow – the botany professor in Cambridge guided and fed Charles' desire to be a great naturalist. Charles enrolled in Henslow's botany class, and often engaged in deep conversation and went on scientific excursions very often with him in the country that soon he was known as the "man who walks with Henslow."

Henslow didn't teach him botany alone but also taught him math and theology, which are subjects required for a degree, as well as botany. Darwin was also introduced to the professor of geology, Adam Sedgwick, by Henslow who fixed the impairment done by Edinburgh to Darwin's interest in the subject, and who took him on a geological tour of Darwin's beloved North Wales, to pursue his interests in the field of geology.

Darwin's deliberations with Henslow comprised every subject of interest to the natural scientist: zoology, entomology, geology, biology, mineralogy, and chemistry, and greatly increased Darwin's knowledge in the subjects he was mostly interested in.

Darwin discovered his first rainforest in Brazil, remembering the experience he calls a "chaos of delight." He rode through the grasslands of Patagonia with gauchos. He found the fossils of huge wiped-out mammals in Uruguay and Argentina, where there wasn't any sign of climate change or quick tragedy that could throw more light on their on why they got extinct. These were a few puzzling findings amongst other discoveries.

Charles returned to England in October 1836, to find out that he was now known because his friend and mentor Henslow had shared his specimens and geological observations with England's top naturalists, who had recognized how successful his science expedition went.

Darwin's immeasurably eager and focused mind led him to the discovery of evolution, the theory of natural selection, the key to the mystery of mysteries, and never overruled the existence of God.

Theodore Roosevelt The First Youngest President Ever

Enthusiasm

Theodore Roosevelt spearheaded one of the most exciting lives in the history of America and it was done with the enthusiasm of a little six-year-old boy.

Theodore Roosevelt was a man of countless interests and gifts. He wrote forty mostly large books. Many didn't believe he would live through the true record of the war, in which his personal adventures assumed so highly, to the pen of some busy scholar safely concealed in his study, who wanted to make sure that Americans had a true picture of the required and magnificent adventure, America's little war with

Spain, that he was honored to have joined beginning from the 1st of July 1898.

As the trumpets sounded as a wake-up call that morning, and the midsummer sun started its rise, which promised a brand new day of scorching heat and dampness for the swamps and jungles of Cuba, an American weaponry bank signaled the beginning of the battle. The commanding officer of the U.S. 2nd Infantry Division – Brigadier General H. W. Lawton, had already started his attack on Spanish forces rooted in fortified locations on a small hill called El Caney. They had a battle plan formed by Brigadier General J. F. Kent's 1st Infantry and Major General "Fightin' Joe" Wheeler's Cavalry Division, where these two other divisions, will move through the thick jungle and hold a spot on the slopes of San Juan Heights. The instruction was for them pending when the 1st

Infantry will end its attack on El Caney and unite with them for a group attack on the greatly fortified Heights.

On the night before the battle, the commander who controlled the invasion force – General William Rufus Shafter, discovered that General Wheeler had broken down with yellow fever as Brigadier General Young who controlled the division's 2nd Brigade had. A regular army physician named Colonel Leonard Wood who is popular for fighting Apaches and received a Medal of Honor for it had to assume Young's brigade due to his illness.

Theodore Roosevelt's entire life, afore and after the Battle of San Juan Heights, was as jam-packed with magnificent activity and striking activities as any life worthy of admiration. Theodore Roosevelt's life before Cuba reveals the most productive, proficient, and cheerful reader embarrassed for priding him or herself on her enthusiasm for life.

Theodore Roosevelt was born in 1858 into the aristocratic Roosevelt family. He was little and sickly, awfully shortsighted, and afflicted by asthma that left him frequently out of breath. Theodore Roosevelt's father was his greatest influence in life and loved him more than anyone else in life. His father usually takes him for rides in his carriage in the cool evening breeze to help his erratic breathing and control his gasping to a minimum level. Theodore Roosevelt had his father's love and attention. His father addressed his son's self-esteem teaching him to defy his physical handicap, calmed his fears, worked on his willpower and physical strength. Theodore Roosevelt gave in to his father's push, he began to exercise and engaged in sports to become stronger and boisterous.

Theodore Roosevelt grew up to become a seasoned historian and promising ornithologist as he loved to wonder at the natural wonders of the world. He amassed a huge collection of natural samplings, mostly birds that he joyfully kills for science and for the pleasure of hunting. He had a distinct hearing that helped him differentiate various birdsongs from a far distance. Theodore Roosevelt loved to swim and fish and hunt and row and hike and ride on horseback any time the opportunity presented itself.

He was a hungry reader, he would read several books daily on any subject he could lay his hands on, from natural history to military science. He erected a library that would compete with that of a university. His memory was second to none, he was known to never forget anything. Many years later, he stunned some dinner guests gathered at a dinner table with his poem recitation he had learned several years ago without making a single mistake.

Before he gained admission into Harvard College, he had knowledge of some subjects that exceeded the knowledge of his professors. When Theodore Roosevelt got to his senior year, he wrote an essay on the naval history of the 1812 War, which turned out to be his initial published book. His thesis was studied at the United States Naval Academy far up the twentieth century. That same season, he lost his dear father; Theodore Roosevelt, Sr., to stomach cancer. He was an emotional wreck and was in deep grief at the time.

He graduated with first-class honors from Harvard in 1880 and got very busy. He attended Columbia law school, this was Theodore Roosevelt studying for the profession he would never exercise. At the age of twenty-three, he became the youngest man ever elected to the New York State Assembly, and he won widespread recognition straightaway to be called a brash and scornfully outspoken whip of corrupt machine politics. Two years after, he won his third term with additional votes than any other legislator accomplished, and was nominated as the leader of the Republican minority.

He returned to New York and politics in 1886, ran for mayor of in 1886, ran for the mayor of New York City, and lost. In 1889, he was selected as a U.S. Civil Service commissioner in the administration of President Benjamin Harrison, he served in the office for six boisterous years and later improved his reputation as campaigning, rhetorically inspiring political reformer who never saw shades of gray, suspected compromise, and rose up every day fortified to do good and prepared to fight evil.

In 1895, he became the Police Commissioner and applied his zeal to reform the notoriously corrupt New York City Police Department. He often walked at night looking for evildoers, some of whom turned out to be policemen.

In 1897, he carried on with his career in the federal government as an assistant secretary of the navy, where he totally overcame the old, miserable secretary, John Long, with the strange, frantic stride of his industry, and his resolve to seize Cuba from Spain's control. He was tense, but he plotted still and got ready for the war he knew would definitely come. When it did come, after the U.S.S. battleship Maine detonated in Havana Harbor – maybe accidentally, the Pacific Fleet, and its commander – Admiral Dewey, were by this time in the Philippines and set to sink the whole Spanish Pacific fleet in the Manila Harbor.

Theodore Roosevelt had already sent them out, got ready for the battle, and didn't bother to tell Secretary Long. Then Roosevelt resigned from the navy, elevated the Rough Riders brigade, trained along with them in Texas, and then went to Cuba to live his normal life.

Over the course of the past twenty years, he had written and printed thirteen books, as well as his powerful four-volume history – The Winning of the West. He wrote twenty-seven more books later and passed on while working on an additional one.

Three months later, he was elected governor of New York after returning to Cuba. Some of his policies didn't sit down well with the party bosses so they got him a ticket to run alongside the then incumbent president – William McKinley who was running for reelection in 1900. The party bosses chose to do so because they thought that putting Roosevelt in a ceremonial office will limit his duties and won't carry out his ambition of clamping their own wings and activities.

In the September of 1901, McKinley was shot by an anarchist named Leon Czolgosz in Buffalo, New York. Theodore Roosevelt had to assume the position of president as the usual custom. He was just forty-two at the time and became the youngest president ever, he rose up a storm of activities and the actualization of his ambition was at his peak.

He was the first president to ride in an automobile, submerge in a submarine, and fly in an airplane, the first to travel outside the country, and the first to invite a leading African American, Booker T. Washington, to dinner at the White House.

Theodore Roosevelt was one of a kind indeed.

The Gift Of A Man Makes Room For Him

Don't lose hope

Once upon a time, there was a young man named Joel, he was born to lovely parents, but there wasn't so much his family could do for him, as they couldn't afford his basic education. So Joel worked twice as hard as he grew up trying his very best. Joel fell in love with making clothes. That is ready-made wear and he kept improving at it.

Joel lived in a poor neighborhood that couldn't afford the kind of clothes he would love to make, so that limited his dream to satisfying the pockets and income of members of his poor community. Joel had another major limitation, he couldn't borrow the sowing machine he had been using on lease anymore as the owner had put it on sale after complaining that Joel hasn't been meeting up with payment early enough. So he needed a sowing machine of how own.

By this time Joel just turned sixteen and felt downcast. He returned how to tell his poor mother that his means of livelihood and the tool that honed his passion had been taken from him, his mother tried to console him but he burst into his room and cried out his eyes, wondering where he will find money to get a new sowing machine and continue to support his family in his own way.

Joel stayed home and continued to draw sketches in his book of various beautiful and elegant styles. He craved to recreate these styles on the sowing machine with fabrics but there weren't any at the moment.

One faithful day, just around their home was a church that Joel loved to sit by just to receive a cool breeze. He always went everywhere with his sketch pad, a drawing pencil, and small chalk. He was lost in his drawing when a lady passed by asking if he lived around the neighborhood. Joel snapped out from his fashion designing world and told the woman he was born in the same neighborhood, then she asked saying, "Forgive me but are you a beggar because I always see you by the side of the road busy on these sheets of paper?" Joel was put off by her question but he thought deeply about how to respond to the woman who could pass for his mother. Joel told her saying, "No ma'am, I am not a beggar, I am a fashion designer, I make clothes of any style. It has always been my passion since I was little. A month ago, the sowing machine I usually use for my work was sold off to someone who could afford it, since then I gave been praying for another machine. So in other not to get rusty, I have been coming out here to sketch various styles because we don't own a fan in our own home and it is always hurt, just in preparation for when God blesses me with my own sowing machine."

The woman was impressed by his spoken English and asked if he went to school Joel said he has never been to school before, but he borrows books from his neighbor's children anytime they return from school. He said he reads wide on every subject and has a small dictionary of his own to check on words he didn't understand the meaning of.

Now this woman was blown away, it showed how impressed she was with how her fair cheeks turned pink. She told Joel that she tested him by asking him if he was a beggar, to see how he would react and she feels very impressed by his composure for a young boy. She also told him that she came to town to supervise a project that she has been around for close to a month and that she always sees him every day on her way back to her lodge and she summoned the courage to ask if he was doing okay.

Joel thanked her for her show of care and told her it was time for him to get back home before his mom begins to fear for his whereabouts.

Joel got home and told his mom about the stranger who had accosted him and they laughed about the whole scenario. The next day, Joel and his parents were having dinner when they heard a knock at their door and his mom answered the door. Lo and behold, it was the lady from the previous day that met Joel at the church, she introduced herself to the family and the family asked that she joined them for dinner of beans and potatoes and she sat to eat with them.

Joel was shocked as to how she knew their home, but he couldn't ask as his father taught him table manners. After dinner, he asked her how she knew their home and she explained that she traced him home just so that she can do what she came to do there on that very day. After that, she called someone over her phone and there was another knock on their door and this time it was the stranger that insisted on answering the door. The family let her, she opened the door and two hefty men were carrying a brand new sowing machine in their home. They struggled to come into the little house as their door was very slim as well. But they managed to bring it in and went back out to bring in more and more food items.

Joel and his parents couldn't accept her gifts as it was quite strange and unusual, the lady told them that they have a great son and that she is doing this for him. She also gave the family some money to hire a private teacher to educate Joel properly as he continues to follow his passion. The family was grateful as their joy knew no bounds.

This singular act of kindness fueled Joel so much that he swung into his craft even more than ever and began to make clothes for all as sundry which fetched him a lot of money. Joel thought that this Good Samaritan was done with his family, but she wasn't. She returned five months after with mobile phones for Joel's parents and a key to a standard fashion design shop for Joel in the city where the rich resided mostly, inside the shop was a room arranged so that Joel can reside there whenever he can't return home to his parents.

That was home Joel's life turned around because he stuck to his dream and remained positive even when life threw shade at him, he remained steadfast.

Wilma Rudolph The Black Gazelle

Excellence

Wilma Rudolph survived racism, poverty, and polio to come to be the fastest woman on earth. Wilma was popularly called La Gazelle Noire, or the Black Gazelle by the whole of Europe. She was an elegant-looking American girl with strong long legs.

Wilma had always recorded successes that keep surprising onlookers after each game. On this particular day, she was faced with a very difficult race which is the 400-meter relay. Many people see it as a challenging one that she can only win with skill and agility.

Wilma anchored her team, running last amongst the four runners from Tennessee State University. Apart from her, the Americans haven't had a lot of success in the 1960 Olympics. The four German runners were seen as the favored ones because they were anchored by the amazingly fast Jutta Heine, who had never lost a race since she arrived in Rome. If the American team were to succeed, the oppressive heat and humidity of the season may be a hindrance. Wilma was twenty-years-old and awarded the model of the fastest woman on earth after medical practitioners said she couldn't make use of her legs to walk.

Wilma Rudolph was born to Blanche and Eddie Rudolph on June 23, 1940, two months earlier than the expected date of delivery. Wilma's mom fell and immediately went into labor, Wilma came out weighing a little over four pounds and wasn't expected to live long. But Wilma survived her early days with the strength and strong will of a horse in spite of her many childhood crises.

Wilma's parents were average people who worked more than one job (Eddie as a railroad porter and handyman, Blanche as a laundress and housekeeper) just to make ends meet. Wilma had twenty-one, other siblings, that their parents had to cater to, so you can imagine how Wilma's home will be during breakfast, lunch, and dinner time.

It wasn't easy to give attention to all their children. The family suffered from poverty, injustice, and segregation in the South. Wilma suffered mumps, measles, chicken pox, and whooping cough before she got to four years old. Colds and the flu constantly afflicted her and she spent most part of her early childhood in bed sick. Blanche nursed her daughter

Wilma using many home remedies, as Clarksville's singular hospital was reserved for only the white people, and there was only one black doctor in town. So, she had to be an expert in administering home remedies to Wilma, in wrapping her in blankets so she can sweat out the fever.

Wilma suffered scarlet fever and pneumonia in her fragile lungs after her fifth birthday. As the symptoms reduced, a more worrisome sign showed was Wilma's left leg starting to twist to the side, which made her unable to move from place to place. When the doctor came and diagnosed Wilma, the result was that she was stricken with polio and may never work again because there was no known cure at the time. This brought a halt to Wilma's entire life, no more school, can't play with her brothers and sisters, and she became more dependent on her already overburdened parents for everything.

Wilma started feeling lonely and dejected like she was constantly sinking with no one to save her, but her family saved her. Their consistent encouragement and care, helped Wilma to rise above her misery, beckon so much strength and courage, and assume an almost phenomenal power of concentration, which made her their miracle child.

Her mom never gave up on her, Wilma and her mother made the journey to Meharry Medical College in Nashville every Saturday, for heat therapy and massages, a two-hour round-trip, riding in the back of the bus as the laws of Jim Crow required. Wilma's mum watched keenly how the doctors worked on Wilma's legs and duplicated the same at home and even taught her older kids how to do the same. Wilma also did personal exercises to strengthen the leg, she would bear the pain with the hope that she will walk again. As time went on, she began to improve and improve.

Wilma learned to walk without crutches and brace. It wasn't a walk in the park, it was difficult but she kept working at it till she proved to her family on her tenth birthday that she had beaten polio once and for all. This she did in church when all her family members were present and they were gladdened. From then on she used her brace sparingly and wore special orthopedic shoes to enable her to walk better with less pain.

Soon Wilma was joining her siblings to run around and play basketball without her special orthopedic shoes. Wilma was healed finally. This healthy version of Wilma was more fun to be with as there was never a dull moment with her. They won the battle.

Wilma intended to play basketball, and she envisioned playing it well, and not just well, but she will be better than other kids.

Wilma was better than the best players on her school's team. She played with a heightened level of speed, agility, talent, and determination than other girls in Clarksville had ever.

When Wilma was sixteen years old, she won the American women's track and field team in the 1956 Olympic Games that were held in Melbourne, Australia.

She failed to endure any of the qualifying heats for the 100- and 200-meter races. But she did qualify for the 400-meter relay. Wilma looked malnourished, and very skinny, mostly bones, arms and legs. Wilma didn't run the anchor leg, but she and her fellow players did well enough to bring home a bronze medal.

When she was twenty years old, she became 138 pounds and moved with some of her college teammates to Rome. Her reputation as a sprinter kept progressing, and she was getting known.

During the rehearsal run for the 100 meters race, Wilma mistakenly stepped into a hole and sprained her ankle. This was a major setback for the Americans. Wilma's ankle got swollen and was discolored, it was later taped and she tested if she could run with it then got ready for the race.

Wilma had long graceful strides, she ran elegantly and relaxed as though she wasn't using up maximum energy with each stride. The way Wilma races past with so much burst of energy was worth every stare. Wilma had grown into a very tall six feet girl. Her legs, firm and ropey and long, and her noble bearing reminded the spectators at Rome's Olympic Stadium of a gazelle, a particularly graceful, elegant, and fast gazelle. She had a graceful smile and had grown into a beautiful young woman, as well as an athlete for whom the normal superlatives did insufficient justice.

She was calm, self-confident, and strongminded, as she was resting for the big game when her teammate woke her up, but she was born ready.

At the shot, Wilma exploded. In less than a second, she had passed by Jutta Heine, who would end up finishing in third, and Dorothy Hyman of Great Britain, who won the silver. Wilma never looked back. Wilma crossed the finish line eleven seconds later, she had set a world record, but because the wind at her back blew over six miles an hour, a mile and a half over the permissible limit, the record was denied her. This was because no one had ever seen a woman run as fast as Wilma or as elegantly.

The crowd cheered along as she, Wilma! Wilma! Wilma! Rang in the air. The crowd's cheers were deafening and it took some time before they quiet down to allow the medal ceremony to take place.

Many people from different corners of the stadia said "The Star-Spangled Banner" as Wilma and her teammates bowed their heads to receive their gold medals. Wilma was the first American woman to win three gold medals. And she was unarguably the fastest woman on earth.

This is a girl that was stricken with polio, racism, and poverty, and now turned out to be the greatest female athlete of her time, and one of the most adored people on earth. Wilma raced in no other Olympics. She had attained excellence, and she knew it could not be surpassed. So she moved on in life chasing other well-meaning tasks.

The then mayor of Clarksville, who was known to crusade as an affirmed guardian of segregation, wanted to hold a parade to welcome Wilma back home after her most deserving victory. In the bizarre customs of racists, however, the event would be limited to whites only. Wilma refused to take part until the mayor give in and permitted all the people of Clarksville to be present at her parade. Wilma insisted that blacks be allowed to be present at an awards dinner that same night too. They were the first combined public events of that nature in the town's history. Every now and then, Wilma appeared to be more proud of that accomplishment than she ever was of her gold medals.

Wilma was truly a great child, the greatest if you might want to add.

Don't Turn Back!

Aspiration

There was once a great man named Ferdinand Magellan who carried out a heroic move. He served one king and won the assistance of another to chase a dream so huge as the world.

This legend's victory has him immortalized as the first European to walk around the world that wasn't open to us. Ferdinand Magellan goes down in history to hold the greatest feat of seamanship which is a daring and marvelous prize.

Ferdinand Magellan was born in 1480 in the mountainous north of Portugal to average parents. Ferdinand had a brother named Diogo and they were given a place in Lisbon's royal court as pages to Queen Leonor during the same year that Columbus set sail from Spain over places beyond the Atlantic Ocean.

While Ferdinand was still at court, Vasco da Gama had gathered the Cape of Good Hope out of the southern part of Africa and journeyed into the Indian Ocean, heading to India. It was the success stories of many brave explorers that birthed Ferdinand's dreams of becoming a great adventurer.

In 1505, Ferdinand joined the carriage of the first Portuguese governor of India, after serving in that capacity for many years, he became skilled at navigating and a more skilled and brave soldier.

Ferdinand fought several battles off the coast of East Africa and India, he suffered many injuries, was more respected, and increased to the rank of a captain. Ferdinand's dedication and consistency had started to pay off now. In 1511, he fought valiantly for Malacca in a battle in Malaysia, which created Portuguese supremacy in Asia. After the battle, Ferdinand explored the Indonesians, (then it was called the Moluccas, which were then known in Europe as the Spice Islands and they were of great value to the Europeans due to their never-ending supply of nutmeg, pepper, ginger, cinnamon, and cloves.

Europeans took over the trade, and the courts of Europe were safeguarded by valiant soldiers who kept searching for a quicker route to Spice Island.

In 1521, Ferdinand went back to Lisbon and the court of King Manuel I. The next year, he went to Morocco in a prestigious carriage gifted by the Portuguese king, laying siege to Azamor's fortress city. Ferdinand later returned home after delivering Azamor into the hands of the Spanish in 1514.

Ferdinand asked for a raise in his pension but was refused. He then renounced his Portuguese citizenship after Manuel's court constantly held him in low regard. When he was to leave, he knelt to kiss the hands of the sovereign as is the usual custom but Manuel retrieved his hand and turned his back away from him. Ferdinand got the worst humiliation of his life he never ever forgot.

Ferdinand went to serve Manuel's rival in the person of young Spanish king Charles I. Charles. He was far younger than Manuel by thirty years. Charles I. Charles gave Ferdinand arms, ships, and supplies for the dangers that lay ahead during his adventure in life.

A messenger of King Manuel Sebastián Alvares, came with flattery, promises, threats, and insults just to get back Ferdinand's dedication to lead his former native country which is Portugal on a very perilous journey in 1519. Sebastián Alvares warned Magellan that his Spanish crews will never ever submit to the authority of a Portuguese commander, and advised that he let go of his expedition and that it will definitely end up in disrepute or disaster.

Ferdinand loved his aspirations much more than his former patriotism, so he waved off the threats and appeals of the emissary sent by Manuel. Manuel was highly disappointed when his emissary reported to him Ferdinand's show of disloyalty to him and his sheer honor to his new king. King Charles ordered that Ferdinand be watched closely and bring back any news of violations of the king's instructions and any signs of disloyalty from Ferdinand.

Just a little number of the men who went for the expeditions had pure bonds of loyalty to their commander, amongst them were Ferdinand's son

Cristóväo, his Malaysian slave, Enrique, and an Italian voyager and adventurer, Antonio Pigafetta, whom Ferdinand asked that he keeps a secret account of the expedition.

Ferdinand pushed that his orders be followed through without any form of hesitation. Later he heard that King Manuel ordered the dispatch of two Portuguese ships to catch up with him and have him arrested.

Ferdinand took the south route instead in order to avoid being captured, they sailed along the western coast of Africa which was a more risky choice because that route was walking through dangerous and uncharted grounds. After sailing for two weeks on calm waters, the journey's route changed and the crew spent two months in a fleet with bad weather that destroyed some parts of their ships and almost crashed them against the hard sea rocks.

Cartagena and some other Spanish captains planned a rebellion and at a conference aboard the Trinidad, he accused Magellan of doing things in the interest of Portugal when he asked that the fleet be misdirected to pass through another route.

Cartagena was seized at the order of Ferdinand, and he was chained in irons. Cartagena called on his other rebellious folks to kill Ferdinand but they refused to. In the end, he was released and laid off from his duties as a captain. He was later kept confined on board in Victoria when he began to nurse evil things of vengeance against Ferdinand.

Three weeks later after the failed rebellion by Cartagena, Ferdinand's fleet got fortunate as their little armada got to sail safely to their first destination in the

New World, Rio de Janeiro due to the favorable winds. After two weeks, the people got fresh provisions and then the fleet forged ahead to find the slippery passage to the other end of the world. The journey was harder than they all thought, each pathway to the west was surveyed just to thwart the explorers and its eager commander with yet another deadlock.

Worse still, the deeper they sailed into the south, the colder and stormier it became. After 5 months of journeying, Ferdinand ordered his ships to wait out the bad southern winter weather at the harbor of San Julian in Argentina. 5 months after they resumed the journey but disaster struck again as Ferdinand lost three of his best captains who got tired of following his ambition haven suffered greatly from the deadly Antarctic winter, secluded for months and had little food rations which birthed rebellion among the crew and three of his captains wanted to go home.

The crew on board the armada pressed Ferdinand to let them wait out the harsh winter but he declined their requests to enjoy more comfort in Rio de Janeiro. Ferdinand pushed that they continue on their journey and insisted that he will never turn back from his expedition until they have discovered their passage to the west and circulated the world. Ferdinand scolded his Spanish officers and crews for their poor dedication to the cause and courage.

Ferdinand got wind that his Spanish captains planned to rebel against him more gravely, so Ferdinand struck first. After making plans with two other captains of his ships that were still very much loyal to him on how to make the other rebellious captains and the crew confess to wanting to kill him on

Easter Sunday, the 1ˢᵗ of April. He woke up one morning to learn that three of his ships has been overtaken by the rebellious folks, but that didn't deter him from his main purpose, not the bad weather, not the failed explorations, Portuguese pursuers, unfriendly natives, reduced supplies, rebellion, and uncharted waters can discourage him from circumnavigating the world, instead, he'd rather die trying.

Victoria's captain, Mendoza, was the real challenge that Ferdinand had. He refused to surrender so Ferdinand sent off fifteen of his armed men in a longboat secretly to Victoria. When the messenger that Ferdinand sent to Mendoza asked him nicely to surrender and he refused, the messenger slit Mendoza's throat, and the fifteen armed men came out of their hiding in a nearby boat and got the Victorian crew to surrender which ended the rebellion.

The captains of the other ship which rebelled against Ferdinand heard of Mendoza's fate but they were too prideful to surrender. So Ferdinand assigned a spy to cut the anchor cable of the Concepción at nightfall which allowed the ship to drift far towards the range of the Trinidad and gave Ferdinand's trusted men a good view of the ship. On the order of Ferdinand, the Concepción was invaded and the rebels surrendered and the same fate was meted out to those of San Antonio.

Ferdinand made an example of the rebels who captured his ships. He ordered that Mendoza's body be dismembered and spread across on stakes to keep reminding everyone of their fate if they ever think of mutiny. Others were sentenced to death by stoning but they were later granted clemency. The evil captain of the Concepción was slain and beheaded by his own servant's sword while Cartagena and a priest who had plotted with Quesada were abandoned on a deserted small island in the harbor where they will fetch scraps to feed and then will later die out of hunger after starving for several weeks or die by the hands of the hostile natives on the strange island.

Spice Islands were still far away, the Ferdinand Magellan fleets still suffered more terrible times. The strong sea wind reduced Ferdinand's fleet to four ships. In mid-October, the terrible weather and wind separated him from his ships (Concepción and San Francisco) when he told them to explore if the lovely bay they sighted on the eastern coast of South America was the entrance to the slippery strait. The strait was discovered to the great ocean in the west and it was named by the explorers "the Strait of All Saints," later generations to come named it "the Strait of Magellan," after its discovery.

This recent discovery was enough for Ferdinand's crew but it was nothing to Ferdinand. His crew asked that they return back to Spain and return back to find Spice Island on a much later date in the future. Ferdinand refused to disembark on his expedition nor did he agree to leave this journey for the future voyage.

He asked that the ship continue to journey to the prohibited waters of the strait. Some days later, the San Antonio, the biggest of the armada's ships which carried most of its provisions, diverted towards the east and ran towards Spain, home. Ferdinand was helpless to stop the defectors and he continued on his dream of finding Spice Island.

Ferdinand and his crew went through the most treacherous journey on the water ever recorded in the history of voyaging, no wonder it is said to be the most magnificent achievement of seafaring in all of history. His three remaining ships made it through the strait after over a month of surviving the horrors of the deadly winds, treacherous waters, and freezing temperatures. The fleet saw the limitless stretch of the biggest ocean in the world. Ferdinand cried at the sight of such beauty which he named the Pacific (peaceful) Sea formerly called the Western Sea.

It took them three and half months to reach the Philippine Islands from the Pacific Sea which is a vast spread of water. Two months later, Ferdinand's crewmen began to die of starvation, Scurvy, and dehydration. They ate biscuits infested with grubs, ate leather strips from behind the yardarms, ate rats, ate sawdust, and drank unclean water that was unhealthy for human consumption. Their gums swell up so much that it was hard to chew.

They could smell the stench of death as they kept dropping dead one by one, but the crew kept heading to their destination. Eighteen months later on the 4th of March, they had now passed the Pacific Ocean and spotted land ahead. By this time, the men on board were already skeletons walking around, very weak. After surviving the deadly journey and traveling 42,000 miles though famous Columbus only reached 8,000 miles.

Ferdinand was killed by the primitive islanders' warriors called the Lupa Lupa leaving his crew members to sail for the Spice Islands. By then their numbers had reduced and were too few to manage tree ships, so they hastened and burnt the Concepción.

Ferdinand's flagship was blown north facing Japan and it was seized by a Portuguese skilled fighter and lost.

Only the Victoria made it back to Spain with eighteen men on board and it was filled with cloves from the Spice Islands, a fortune great enough to earn the voyage proceeds, in spite of its heavy losses. On the return of Victoria, its captain named Juan Sebastian Del Cano received the accolades meant for Ferdinand Magellan. He was called the man who went around the world for Spain. Can you imagine the turn of events as another man inherited the wealth, fame, and honor of the real hero Ferdinand Magellan after all his steadfastness and aspirations?

Several years after was Ferdinand Magellan recognized as the real hero after Antonio Pigafetta published the real events of the perilous because he secretly recorded the events of the voyage through his journal notes as instructed by Ferdinand when the journey began.

Antonio Pigafetta wrote about the captain he had come to admire above all other men and made sure Ferdinand got immortalized, writing in his publication saying; "In the midst of the sea he was able to endure hunger better than we. Most versed in nautical charts, he knew better than any other the true art of navigation, of which it is certain proof that he by his genius, and his intrepidity, without anyone having given him the example, knew how to attempt the circuit of the globe which he had almost completed."

You'd conclude that the tale of Ferdinand ended not so well because he didn't live to enjoy the rewards of his accomplishments but we can benefit from it. But know that without Ferdinand Magellan, none of us would know about the Pacific Sea nor the Spice Island ever existed. He stayed on course in the presence of turmoil, discouragement, and betrayal. Today we can enjoy the fruit of his labor.

Conclusion

As kids you have to create our own paths and uphold your right to be yourself; Dare to be different in whatever you do and do not try to imitate anyone. Live your own life and follow your true star.

" It's ok to be different, the climate is not the same in every mind." – Bangambiki Habyarimana

Printed in Great Britain
by Amazon

24984613R00075